Gone

The Missing Years of Bjorn Esterday

Book 01

Bubble

Year 2030

Wynter Sommers

This work is registered with the UK Copyright Service, in accordance with the Copyright, Designs and Patents Act 1988 All rights reserved 284718038 for

GONE: The Missing Years of Bjorn Esterday

USA Copyright © 2015 GJ dePillis
© TXu002023789 and TXu002010532 / 2016

Library of Congress Control Number: 2021936597

Published by Pure Force Enterprises, Inc.
California, USA
Since 2002

INGRAM
INGRAM® Distribution

DEDICATION

To those who feel strongly about truth, justice, and the integrity of America; your honorable actions make us proud.

To those who wonder if their daily choices matter; your small decisions impact generations to come.

To those everyday people who don't think they have what it takes; your perseverance and strive for the extraordinary, makes the impossible a reality.

To those who have failed; know you will make it and tomorrow will be better.

Your dreams today become our future tomorrow.
Thank you for everything you do.

Bjorn Esterday
Was Not Born Yesterday
Series

Firebrand (15 Volumes+Conversation Station Book)
Edges (9 Stories +Conversation Station Book)
Gone (18 Stories + Conversation Station Book + Log book)

Bjorn EDGES Series
EDGES Book 1-Swift Encounter
EDGES Book 2-Rousing Attack
EDGES Book 3-One Foot Under
EDGES Book 4-Earthshake
EDGES Book 5-Broken String
EDGES Book 6-Key Witness
EDGES Book 7-Who is She?
EDGES Book 8-Vanish
EDGES Book 9-Chase or Die

Bjorn Series Alternate Reading Plan

1st	Edges Book 1	25th	Gone Book 11
2nd	Edges Book 2	26th	Firebrand Vol 10
3rd	Gone Book 1	27th	Gone Book 12
4th	Firebrand Vol 1	28th	Gone Book 13
5th	Edges Book 3	29th	Firebrand Vol 11
6th	Firebrand Vol 2	30th	Gone Book 14
7th	Gone Book 2	31st	Gone Book 15
8th	Gone Book 3	32nd	Firebrand Vol 12
9th	Firebrand Vol 3	33rd	Gone Book 16
10th	Gone Book 4	34th	Gone Book 17
11th	Firebrand Vol 4	35th	Firebrand Vol 13
12th	Gone Book 5	36th	Gone Book 18
13th	Gone Book 6	37th	Gone Book 19
14th	Gone Book 25-	38th	Edges Book 5
Longfellow's Journal		39th	Edges Book 6
15th	Edges Book 4	40th	Gone Book 20
16th	Firebrand Vol 5	41st	Gone Book 21
17th	Gone Book 7	42nd	Edges Book 7
18th	Firebrand Vol 6	43rd	Gone Book 22
19th	Gone Book 8	44th	Firebrand Vol 14
20th	Firebrand Vol 7	45th	Firebrand Vol15 (End)
21st	Gone Book 9	46th	Edges Book 8
22nd	Firebrand Vol 8	47th	Edges Book 9(End)
23rd	Gone Book 10	48th	Gone Book 23
24th	Firebrand Vol 9	49th	Gone Book 24(End)

ACKNOWLEDGMENTS

We acknowledge those who actively build peace. We acknowledge all the selfless talent which contributed to creating meaningful tokens of consideration and sharing. We acknowledge that every person has a daily choice of right or wrong... and we thank you for choosing the right, good, honorable path filled with integrity because that is the difficult and brave path. Small choices today become lasting monuments of loving hope tomorrow.

CONTENTS

0 Setting

Locations

- **AromaX**: City of fragrance & fashion

- **Courtly City**: City of solar & other technical products. Bjorn Esterday and Sarah Paradise live here.

- **Brio**: Underwater village

Characters

- **Otto Mattick**: One of the sibling rulers of AromaX

- **Pip**: Son of Skipper Courtly

- **Zor**: Chief prosecutor of Brio

- **Pat**: Resident in Brio

- **Watson**: Charismatic public speaker

0 PREFACE

The taste of Freedom is sweet, once obtained, after piercing through oppression. What must it take to be a sharp investigative reporter in a dwindling quiver of corporate owned media releases? Here we pick up on Bjorn Esterday, reporter at the Daily Memo, who vanished for years, leaving Sammy Scribe, his editor, dumbfounded by another of Bjorn's seemingly cavalier abandonments. Sarah Paradise longed to see her friend again in spite of his sudden apparent loss of integrity. Bjorn's absence gnawed at her, yet Courtly City trained their residents to just accept fate... but would Sammy? Could Sarah?

Always urgently placating the influential elites of Courtly City, editor Sammy Scribe still waivered desperately between conforming in speech and thought to harkening to that faint echo of integrity which begged him to search for the truth as to what really happened to Bjorn Esterday, his very best reporter. To which force would Sammy yield?

Even while trying to acquiesce to the demands of compliance from Courtly City's influentials, Sammy sends Bjorn on a benign assignment, one far beneath the skills of his reporter, yet Bjorn obediently obeys, yet...vanishes, leaving Sammy in the lurch.

But did Sammy willingly hide Bjorn to protect him? Or did he get rid of Bjorn because the reporter's inquisitive nature had finally ruffled too many elitist feathers? .

Sarah has learned her lesson in that doing what is right- because it is the right thing to do - sometimes brings immediate punishment, yet can reveal long term rewards. Does Sarah understand the cost of being free? Why some would die for the chance to make their own life choices? Why living in a just world is a luxury? What is the price of being free? Insidious schemes start with one small bad choice. If left unchecked, the consequences could slither silently around you, then suddenly tighten to a steely grip and pull you down leaving you helpless to do anything but succumb. Catch evil early before it grows too powerful; before it prevents you from living your destiny.

Is "freedom" simple? Must freedom be carefully maintained and safeguarded? If one pursues freedom, can new skills be gained from the struggle?

1 CHAPTER 01: (2030) BRIO: COURTROOM: BJORN DREAMING

Bjorn jolted awake to the smell of metal and saltwater. Muscles aching. Eyes dry. Sammy Scribe, his boss, must have sent Bjorn on an assignment.

Was he on a boat? There was no sound of lapping waves. No gentle rocking of a vessel on water. Sometimes his Daily Memo Newspaper assignments wove through his dreams. Was he dreaming about boats? His head pounding, he still heard a low-pitched droning hum. Unfamiliar. Mechanical. He fought to open his eyes and move his arms only to find his wrists restrained.

Bjorn's head was swimming. Had he been captured by AnCors? Were they going to torture him? Sell him into slavery? Kill him? He passed out again and now saw the face of Sarah Paradise as he helped her onto his horse. They rode through the black steel and sparkling crystal towers of Courtly City to Library. Children came running out and waved. Would he ever see her again?

Then, Bjorn felt a kick as a man in golden robes shouted above him.

"I am Zor!" the man proclaimed, "Chief prosecutor of Brio." He waved his golden robed arms and pointed at Bjorn.

"You are a murderer!"

Bjorn was strapped into a large chair in an elevated defendant's box in front of a solemn blank-faced jury. Everything seemed to float in a pale blue haze. Blue. What a contrast to Courtly City. He felt as if he were somehow suspended in a fishbowl.

Zor raised his arms again. The jury, as if hypnotized, stood in unison, all dressed in blue jumpsuits. Zor lowered his arms and the expressionless jury sat back in their seats.

Bjorn sputtered a curt laugh and blurted, "Crazy dreams!"

Bjorn Esterday spoke louder than he had intended. He shut his eyes tight in an attempt to clear away the image of a seated jury and a man in long flowing robes.

The robed man declared, "That 'crazy dreams' comment, Your Honor, justifies the reason Lou Pole Linden asked the defendant to be here. It proves that this man... this man who is named Otto Mattick, sitting in that defendant's chair, murdered the victim, Charlie Horse."

Bjorn opened his mouth, to protest, but couldn't speak.

The iridescent grey blue room grew dark on one side. A shadow steadily crept across the jury. They did not seem to notice. Then, Bjorn looked up. Above him, a shaft of light streamed down from somewhere outside, through the transparent curved walls and ceiling of this place. The light, which had danced languidly around inside this great room, now was becoming oddly obscure.

Bjorn abruptly realized they were all under water. This iridescent courtroom was inside a glass dome! As he gazed up into that beam of sunshine through the transparent ceiling, he saw the belly of a whale as the huge sea creature swam overhead.

Eyes darting to the man in the golden robes, Bjorn called out, "Who? Who are these guys?"

Zor fumed, "Dr. Lou Pole Linden? Charlie Horse? To whom do you refer, Mr. Mattick?"

Bjorn snapped, "All of them. Who are they? What have they to do with me? My name is Bjorn Esterday... Not Otto Mattick. I don't know those other people."

Bjorn Esterday fought to remember.

Zor clenched his fists and demanded, "We are waiting, Otto Mattick, for your statement as to the last thing you recall... If you are telling the truth, you should not need to think this long."

Bjorn sputtered, "My boss, Sammy Scribe. I'm a reporter... Sammy gave me an assignment to write for our newspaper, the Daily Memo. He wanted an article about Watson. Sammy promised me the contact information of a woman I had met a couple of weeks ago... in exchange for writing the article."

Zor paused and then stepped up to the judge's bench.

"Your Honor... was there an article printed about the Courtly City Watson convention?"

Bjorn saw the floating balloon head drift down in front of him. It was now that he recognized the face of Watson.

The face of this 'Watson', the man himself, projected onto the balloon, now floated in front of Bjorn. The Watson balloon peered closely at Bjorn, closely examining his features.

Bjorn realized that this balloon was a two-way mode of communication. Watson would be safe, probably somewhere up on the surface, while using the balloon as a conduit to observe and interact with the people of this underwater court.

The balloon judge face of Watson drifted away from Bjorn and floated toward Zor to mutter, "I'll check." The face image projected on the balloon abruptly vanished, but the balloon itself remained suspended in mid-air.

After a moment of total silence, the face re-appeared onto the surface of the balloon, which floated back toward Bjorn.

The balloon head of Watson barked, nose crinkled with disgust, "There has been no article printed in the Daily Memo. No publicity! None!"

Bjorn blurted, "But I sent it in. It was very opinionated! My work usually is. Maybe they didn't print it because..."

Zor raised his arm and pushed his palm into Bjorn's face, "Silence!"

The balloon head floated away and took its place again hovering over the judge's bench. The judge announced, "Several citizens are watching this trial, now. That is very good. Continue, Zor."

Zor looked around and saw a growing number of faces pressing against the transparent walls.

Zor smiled to himself. He knew for every face visible, he could look forward to being financially well-rewarded. He addressed the jury.

"Ladies and gentlemen of the Jury of Brio, listen carefully," Zor explained, "Frequently, when a defendant suffers from compound guilt, the stress forces him to develop an alternate personality. It appears that we are fortunate enough to witness this entertaining twist in our murder trial."

"I'm not Otto Mattick, I tell you!" Bjorn exclaimed, "I've committed NO murder!"

"Eject him into the waters for his insolent outbursts!" bellowed the judge-head of Watson projected onto the balloon.

"No!" Bjorn defended, "All right. If you want to call me Otto Mattick, I'll cooperate. I don't need to be ejected and become dinner to some fish out there... OK. I'll answer your questions..."

"And," Zor checked, "Will you follow the rules of this court?"

"Are these rules written down anywhere?" Bjorn asked a tad flippantly.

"I make the rules of this court and change them as I deem fit," Zor replied.

"Actually," the floating judge-head, or Bonitor, added, "I make the rules..."

Zor bowed to the balloon, "Yes, of course, Your Honor. Of course, I uphold your rules. Yes. Thank you, Your Honor..."

The floating balloon judge-head ordered, "Zor. Carry on."

12

Zor smiled and gave another deep bow and then stood erect and approached Bjorn.

"You claim," Zor started, "You were a reporter up on the surface world where they see sky. Now that we know there was no article printed about the Watson convention in Courtly City, do amuse the court by telling us how you got the writing assignment in the first place, Mr. Mattick."

Bjorn took a deep breath and recalled Sammy Scribe, his boss, shouting. Bjorn remembered pacing Sammy's messy office, walls cluttered with digital photos changing constantly to highlight all the famous people Sammy had encountered in his long career as Editor-In-Chief at the Daily Memo newspaper.

"My boss told me what I was writing was rubbish. Too bland. Had no heart. He told me that if I continued to voice my opinion, it would eventually infuriate the Top Brass..."

"The Administrators in Courtly City have power over the education system and Sammy Scribe was worried they were probably also planning to bully their way into his newspaper. There was a woman who was socializing herself up the ladder. He didn't want any reporter to write an inflammatory article which might offend the Administrators, who would force him to cut staff."

Zor asked, "So you and this Sammy Scribe on the surface had an altercation? A fight?"

The jury murmured anxiously amongst themselves. The cloud of excitement intensified as this small group hoped for juicy details to give them a jolt of adrenaline they could brag about with their friends. Bjorn, observing their reactions, realized they fed off extreme emotional swings. He wondered if his situation was feeding the emotional hunger of this Brio audience.

"Not a fight," Bjorn snapped, not wanting to satisfy the crowd by turning his plight into some form of entertainment. "Sammy observed I was frustrated because I was not able to write facts… to warn the citizens of Courtly City about real issues."

Zor interrupted, "Courtly City has a ruling family. Two children if I recall…"

"Yeah," Bjorn nodded, "The kids from the ruling family…"

"Ace and Pip?" Zor prodded.

"Yeah, those kids," Bjorn agreed, "liked the comical images section of the newspaper, but needed to make the other stories more entertaining so they'd read it. News. Facts. I guess they were boring. Sammy said the Administrators told him to not print anything which could depress the readers."

Zor shot back with a pointed finger as if he had triumphantly discovered a truth, "Meaning the children of the ruling family decided the fate of Sammy Scribe's Daily Memo newspaper?"

Bjorn nodded to affirm Zor's question, then closed his eyes briefly as the jury discussed his statement. Zor was pondering what to ask next.

Bjorn recalled Sammy Scribe waving his hands around. They were badly in need of a manicure. He remembered Sammy looking down from his office window onto the black streets of Courtly City. The smart roads were designed to absorb solar energy and recharge the wheeled vehicles.

Bjorn had wanted to write about adding in a horse lane on each side of the road so that manure could be collected under the street and transported to a conversion plant to create energy or make fertilizer for the fields of the Earth Farmers in Courtly City.

Sammy said no.

He said he agreed with Bjorn, but reminded Bjorn they wouldn't have the Daily Memo horse stable if it weren't for Bjorn breaking that story. The one about starving wild horses being forced to wander down into the city to search for natural fodder.

That's where Bjorn introduced Sammy Scribe to the Overflow Barn Groomsman.

16

When it was time to retire the horses from the Daily Memo horse stable, they'd be returned to the Overflow Barn. Bjorn had worked with a wrangler who rounded them up from the wild. The lack of vegetation was being caused by the continued dumping of toxic waste from one of Skipper Courtly's favorite companies, the Mayfounder Foundation.

Bjorn remembered that as Sammy gazed out onto the ebony and crystal architecture of Courtly City, he reminded Bjorn Esterday that they had recently lost a great leader in the train wreck death of Jack Courtly.

Bjorn recalled Sammy saying, "...because the people out there are depressed by the news that Jack Courtly, the leader of Courtly City, here, died on that train with his family...with his wife, Queenie and kid, Ace. Bjorn and the citizens of Courtly City became nervous about Jack's brother, Skipper Courtly, taking over."

Skipper Courtly, empty headed, party-hard, easily bribed...

That was the new ruler of Courtly City, the new absolute Director of the Courtly City Corporation.

"The Administrators don't want another negative story... You need to write something uplifting."

The tall towers of Courtly City used black components by design to aid in the conversion of solar power into energy to power the buildings. Crystal accents worked as a focus of that energy so light would shine out and illuminate the streets when night fell on the city. Highly polished grey steel door knobs and kick plates gleamed against the dark somber solar absorbers.

These images comforted Bjorn. It reminded him of home...Courtly City, where he could see sky.

Zor snapped Bjorn out of his dream world with the statement, "So, Mr. Mattick, even in your fantasies of being a reporter on the surface, you were not good enough to get a story printed. What motivated you to cover the Watson convention?"

"I told you!" Bjorn clenched his teeth in frustration. These questions from this Zor... in this strange underwater world were irritating, confusing and even frightening when Bjorn contemplated and evaluated how much power this Zor appeared to have. "Sammy Scribe got alerted that I was searching for a woman... a school teacher I had met at the train station ...on the day the Leader of our city, Jack Courtly, died in a train accident."

Bjorn recalled Sammy perched on the corner of his desk, which was so cluttered, he had to sit on top of his overflowing in-basket. As Sammy moved to sit more comfortably, he accidentally spilled his beverage, which he sopped up with the sleeve of his sweater which hung askew over the back of his chair.

Sammy had sent Bjorn to cover another story the day Bjorn Esterday met Sarah Paradise. Bjorn had left Sarah at Library surrounded by excited children pleased to see Sarah arrive on a horse, as if out of a storybook.

There was something about Sarah's character, which appealed to Bjorn. Her insistence on keeping her promise to some school children to tour Library that day. She showed compassion, even to those who could not further her career. Bjorn knew that most people would only develop a friendship if there was something in it for them. Sarah was different.

Bjorn had left her at Library with the school children. He had galloped away, assuming he would see Sarah again.

But he never did.

Inspired by Sarah's kindness to the young ones, Bjorn's heart was touched when he was en route to his next assignment.

He heard that Watson and his groupies were evaluating the venue of the Courtly City Convention Center to see if they could fill seats in the city's huge auditorium.

Out of curiosity, Bjorn had ridden his horse to the Convention Center to observe how the astonishingly successful con-artist Watson and his team of crooks conducted their set up. Bjorn was shocked to see that some of Watson's staff had found a few stray dogs near the trash outside, looking for food. The uniformed Watson team had cornered the dogs, kicking them, for amusement...

Bjorn couldn't catch what they were saying, but heard them laughing. Bjorn had galloped over, slipped off his horse and shouted at the two workers to stop harming stray animals.

The dogs ran away, scared.

Knowing they were still hungry, Bjorn called a contact, the Groomsman at the Overflow Barn, whom Bjorn had interviewed when he rescued the wild horses and worked to get them dedicated to Sammy Scribe's reporter staff. It was those horses which resided in the Daily Memo stables at the Newspaper. The Groomsman said he would help Bjorn rescue the stray dogs.

Bjorn recalled the long process of catching the dogs and using horse lead ropes as leashes to keep the canines from running away. Bjorn had purchased sausages from the concession stand of the Convention Center and used that to feed the hungry dogs. Although the Watson convention had not been set up, yet, Bjorn already had a low opinion of Watson's staff.

When the Groomsman arrived, he told Bjorn he could take the dogs to a vet for a health examination and then knew of a place where the dogs could be adopted by somebody he would contact.

Bjorn wanted to make sure the dogs would get to a good home. The Groomsman assured Bjorn that this fellow used to live in AromaX and had experience with being a pack leader. The owner the Groomsman had heard of already had a Jack Russel Terrier and a Belgium Malinois.

Bjorn told the Groomsman that although Bjorn lived in an apartment, he still wanted a guarantee that these dogs would end up in a good place... if not, then to return them to Bjorn. Bjorn gave the Groomsman Bjorn's contact at the Daily Memo paper. The Groomsman had agreed.

Bjorn had then kneeled down to pet the soft fur of another one of the strays, a black Labrador Retriever, covered with the dust of the streets.

Bjorn had said, "Hey, good bye dusty guy." Bjorn didn't know that later on this dog's new owner would name the dog 'Dustin'. He also patted the head of a very tired looking poodle, once white, and now neglected and splattered with mud. Bjorn had asked the Groomsman, "Poodles need regular grooming and this one is smart. Took a while to corner it on Tustin street." Bjorn gently touched the matted and dirty fur of this stray, then asked the Groomsman, "Can you make sure the home you send this dog to will groom it properly?"

The Groomsman nodded.

Bjorn had gotten back on his horse to make it to the location Sammy Scribe had sent him to investigate. He was several hours late, but still got a story...

a very bland story, much to Sammy's chagrin. Bjorn considered the fact that if he had not been exposed to Sarah's earnest compassion for those innocent children at Library, perhaps he would not have shown such dedication to rescuing a few stray dogs. But, he was glad he had been able to give the lost animals a second chance at survival.

Something startled Bjorn. He abruptly shook his head, and was mildly surprised to find he was still in this absurd courtroom. Still dreaming?

Zor was addressing the jury.

"Jury of Brio, this is a rare trial indeed. The defendant names a woman. Is it possible this woman was an unrequited romance?

"The defendant has created a full alternate identity to avoid taking the blame for the murder of our fellow resident Charlie Horse."

Zor gazed out the transparent wall and saw that some faces had left only to bring back curious friends. The numbers of viewers of the trial were increasing.

Zor approached the bench, "Shall we recess or continue, Your Honor?"

The floating head of Watson smiled, "Do continue."

Bjorn shook a lock of hair from his eyes. He tested the restraints on his wrists. His muscular forearms rippled with tension. His jaw clenched. He only drew solace from the fact that he was now fully awake and not dreaming. He did not know how far beneath the surface of the ocean this was all taking place. He quickly reasoned cooperation was probably his best chance of survival.

Zor asked, "Tell us about this woman."

Bjorn hesitated, then said simply, "Sarah something was her name. Sammy Scribe had sent me to the train station to cover a story. In Courtly City, when the Soldier Police, the SPs, announce an ACA, Anti Corporate Activity Alert, the only mode of transportation we are allowed to use is trains. That day, however, they suspected AnCors were inside the train station, so they had to lock down all the entrances. That meant that Sarah, the school teacher, couldn't get to meet her class at Library. They were taking a field trip...so I gave her a ride on my Daily Memo issued horse. I tried to contact her later, but the Administrators had moved her to another location. Sammy Scribe said he knew where."

Zor prodded, "So is this a love triangle? Did Sammy Scribe admire your new school teacher friend? Is that why you fought with him?"

Bjorn shook his head, "I didn't fight with Sammy. Sammy said he knew that I tried and failed to find Sarah. He said he knew Sarah didn't have the money to get a comm, but he had a way to contact her. He would give me that information only if I covered the Watson convention. After that I would take my vacation and come back ready to write content for the Daily Memo which would not offend the Administrators. Sammy was worried that the Administrators would force him to cut back on staff if any of the reporters printed something which did not agree with Administrator viewpoints."

Zor asked, "How is it this Sammy Scribe could locate her but you, an investigative reporter, could not?"

Bjorn replied cautiously since he didn't want to betray Sammy, "Um. Sammy said he got hold of...uh...some old information. I don't know anything else. Sammy basically told me to take my vacation and then return ready to write non-controversial content."

Bjorn was satisfied this answer would preserve Sammy's secret that he had discovered an old SP database so he could know where to send his reporters. Every registered HIB, or Holographic Identification Badge, kept continual track of all the citizens of Courtly City.

"So, what are your thoughts on Watson?" Zor challenged.

The balloon head of Judge Watson's face floated down to better observe Bjorn's reaction.

"Um," Bjorn sighed, "Frankly, I'm not a big fan of using the words 'positive' in the same sentence as 'energy' and 'universe'. But, if you motivate people, good for you. Just not for me personally... the point is I covered the Watson show..."

"Show?" Zor snapped with disapproval.

"Convention... Watson Convention..." Bjorn corrected, suppressing a grin. "I covered it objectively to get Sarah's contact info."

Zor challenged, "Which is where? Where is this Sarah contact information?"

Bjorn looked around, his wrists still restrained, "I don't think I have it anymore..."

Zor smiled at the jury, "How convenient that you are unable to even verify the existence of this woman. More fantasies, Jury of Brio. This man, Otto Mattick speaks entertaining lies."

Bjorn grimaced, "Not lies. I recall some

details. Like when Sammy and I struck the deal with a simultaneous bow. We agreed that I'd write the piece, then get refreshed with time away, and then write prose about nothing. With a smile. I agreed."

Zor commanded Bjorn, "Then give me some detail of what you remember...anything at all..."

Bjorn quickly replied, "I remember a coworker, Maria Carina, was going to cover the story, but she was overloaded. I remember seeing her talking with other reporters from inside Sammy's office. People were asking her questions and she almost slipped in a spilled drink from another coworker, nearly knocking over a stack of papers headed to Library archives. That's why I took the assignment. Maria Carina already had her hands full. Sammy even commented that he'd have to move the stack of old editions inside his office from now on. Then I went to the Courtly City Convention Center."

Zor instructed, "Now tell the jury in

detail what transpired once you arrived at the Convention Center..."

Bjorn searched back in his memory, and then began to detail how he stopped on the street in front of the massive Courtly City Convention Center.

He recalled watching as the great heavy metal doors automatically parted to admit him and the small crowd which had also gathered. The doors closed behind them once they were inside.

The Watson entertainment was already in progress for the first audience which were in attendance for the initial show.

The group, which had just entered with Bjorn, disappeared into the auditorium to join the early crowd.

Bjorn chose to linger out in the entrance area.

"We are so pleased the universe led you to us today." One woman approached Bjorn speaking softly in overly powdery tones. She put on a huge smile as she held out her hand for Bjorn's HIB. "Your Holographic Identification Badge, please?"

Bjorn unclipped it and handed it over as she scanned it and then printed out a name-tag for him to wear.

She explained, while still smiling, "He's already started, but later all carbon units will unite and partake of our meal which will bring you into consciousness, let you forget all of your past worries, and permit you to bond with your new family."

Bjorn asked, trying to suppress a smile, "Are you part of my new family? Or will I transform to look just like you?"

She pointed to what she wore and tried to explain, "You will receive a similar garment once you are inducted, and then when you are transformed, you will get one which will symbolize the unity of your family."

"Huh. Okay." Bjorn smiled again and now followed the lighted arrows, which pointed him toward the main hallway.

First, he had to pass through the temporary booths each manned by a person clothed in that garment identical to the one worn by the first woman he met. They all smiled and followed him with their eyes. They all wished him peaceful passage and offered him some free trinket while quickly following up with today's bargain offer. Bjorn couldn't decipher their words. He walked quickly between the rows of booths. As they called gently to him, he noted each of them followed exactly the same pattern of words to the point where their speeches overlapped incoherently.

They interacted with almost military precision. First, greet Bjorn as "brother". Then, hand him something, which Bjorn politely declines. Next, they offer him some discount for their product, and then warn him the discount is set to expire by the end of the Great Watson's speech.

Bjorn Esterday, investigative reporter, was relieved to have survived the gauntlet of merchants and finally end up in the back of the famous auditorium. It was overfilled with people enraptured by the man with the large screens behind him so people in the back, like Bjorn himself, could see Watson's every move, hear every word.

Bjorn lurked at the rear of the great room in the shadows, near the table where mounds of untouched food were waiting to be consumed. Bjorn's eyes were drawn to the cool bowl of iced drinks, containers of sweet desserts, and various tasty buffet morsels. He realized at that moment he had not yet had lunch.

Alas, however, he had to focus on his assignment. He extracted his note-taking device from his blazer pocket, and immediately began writing up his observations, in order to quickly RedMail the completed story to his boss.

He smirked to himself knowing that his "redacted mail", his "RedMail", would be read and probably censored by some Administrator, who would decide if Sammy Scribe, the Editor of the Daily Memo, should even see it. Bjorn was determined to get this job done, and be out of there, before some Watson followers forced him into one of those ridiculous garments.

Bjorn leaned forward.

The man on the stage moved around taking large steps and making broad sweeping arm gestures as he pronounced each word with dramatic intensity.

"I am Watson, I said to him." The speaker continued his story. "And yet he claimed he had never heard of me."

The audience laughed. Bjorn presumed this speaker must be Watson himself.

The speaker went on.

"But I saw his empty pain and loneliness. I shared with him how he could get a second chance. He could wipe away his past mistakes, his past life, if he wanted to. He'd embrace a future created by him, where he was the captain of his own ship...and he accepted my invitation to embrace the

'Erase'."

The audience burst into cheers and Bjorn heard phrases like "Welcome brother" and "Embrace the Erase".

The speaker emphasized, "He was astounded that for such a teensy weensy investment, he could enhance his chance."

The crowd shouted overjoyed, "enhance my chance", they repeated. Some in the crowd threw in "embrace the erase, embrace the erase." And then together they all cheered and chanted, "Improve me... ImpMi... Improve... ImpMi..."

Bjorn stopped himself from remembering the chant of "improve me", concatenated to the simplistic "ImpMi", and turned to directly address Zor.

"Your Zorness, after that, I wrote and RedMailed my story to my boss at the Daily Memo. That's about it..."

What Bjorn had not shared with the court of Brio was that when he had tried to RedMail Sammy, his device was not getting a signal from where he stood inside the conference room. Bjorn knew he'd have a better chance of getting connectivity once he left the cavernous auditorium.

Bjorn had silently mused to himself, "Sammy will never print more than the first four or five paragraphs. I keep putting in my opinion. I guess I really do need to take a holiday."

Bjorn remembered back to that last day as the Watson speaker droned on. Bjorn recalled that he had quietly slipped out of the audience. Once in the hall, he had casually meandered over to the buffet table, and swiped a morsel of food along with a small pre-packaged can of punch before he stepped into the hallway.

Fortunately, none of the attentive overly cheerful brotherly Watson staff witnessed Bjorn disturb the perfectly arranged food before everybody else got the chance to sample it at the Watson official snack time. And the wrapped goodies created bulk on only one side of

Bjorn's jacket.

Bjorn could still hear Watson's voice as the man continued to address his flock.

"Distilling your consciousness will allow you to select your ImpMi, to live in a city with no crime, wonderfully fresh food, fresh air, no disease and no pain. You can be transformed to the life you've always dreamed of. Your ImpMi with your memories, your soul, your thoughts will survive the decay of whatever ails your current body."

The audience, mesmerized by Watson's promises, again began to chant, "Improve me, ImpMi. Improve me ImpMi. Improve me ImpMi. ImpMi. ImpMi. ImpMi...." The sound of drums beat in time to the chant.

Bjorn recalled, Watson had smiled for a long moment at his audience before he continued.

"This former military technology has now been harnessed to make you find a better you. An improved you...and me. Escape your worldly problems and live a fresh life with your personalized ImpMi. Let me hear you say, 'My imagination will open doors to my improved me. My ImpMi.'"

The crowd stopped chanting, "Improve me ImpMi" and started the earnestly muttered pledge of, "my imagination will open doors to my improved me. My ImpMi..." Watson added on hastily, "Payments are easy and automatically extracted from your credits".

Bjorn put on a mindless smile as his eyes met one of the Watson staff standing at the door.

Bjorn asked, "Which way to the men's?" while concealing the food and drink he had just collected in one pocket.

The Watson staff door keeper pointed down the hall toward the men's toilet, and handed Bjorn a hand-held activated display screen, then said, "It's a very easy payment plan. I have forms here you can complete. Just press there."

"Thanks, I'll think about it," Bjorn said pushing it away.

The Watson door-keeper was insistent about hitting a button on the screen of the small device as a holographic image of a form asking for Bjorn's personal details, abruptly floated above it.

"Today only," the door-keeper enthusiastically urged. "Just sign here and we do the rest of the work. Even if you die, your ImpMi contains your distilled consciousness, so your memories will live on. It's like cheating death and living the life you wanted but could never have. We have several packages and products to select from. Limited offer. No payments for ninety days. Today only. Just enter your bank account there and sign here."

Bjorn wrinkled his nose and said, "When I come back... I've got some personal business to attend to and I just won't be able to recall my bank account until its taken care of."

"Oh, right. Sorry. Down the hall that way," the Watson door-keeper whispered, then resumed his blank stare on the speaker as if he were being nourished by the words of Watson.

Once outside in the corridor, Bjorn glanced up and down the empty hallway to make sure he would not have any witnesses to his impromptu snack, then he popped the morsel into his mouth, gulped down the drink and hid the cup in a nearby plant to conceal the evidence of his hunger from any of the overly enthusiastic Watson staff.

Then, Bjorn made further adjustments to his note taking device, finally received a signal, and sent the article off to Sammy, realizing most of the negativity would be edited out.

Bjorn muttered to himself, "I am not going back in there...so..."

Sammy Scribe had just sent Bjorn the new location for Sarah Paradise in return for the story. "Good man, Sammy," Bjorn muttered as he mapped out the best path to the school where Sarah Paradise was now employed. He could hop on a train or take a long walk.

The doors of the convention hall

opened up. Out scurried a man with mousey coloring and wire framed glasses.

"You all right?" he asked Bjorn. Bjorn assessed the man and concluded this was another attendee, not yet inducted and not yet clad in the uniform of a Watson disciple.

Bjorn shoved his device in his pocket and started to walk away, not answering this man.

The man repeated to Bjorn, "You need to sit down or something?"

"I'm fine," Bjorn replied, "You from Courtly City?" Bjorn now realized focusing was difficult. He couldn't see the features of this man's face. The room seemed to see-saw and sway...

The man reached over and yanked Bjorn's conference nametag from him and tried to pronounce it. The man said, "Bish-jon? John? Beejay-on? Sort of. I came from AromaX because my boss needed to see this Watson guy here at the Courtly Convention Center."

"Bjorn," Bjorn corrected, "Name's pronounced Bjorn Esterday, reporter at the Daily...What's your name?" Bjorn managed to say before his eyes rolled back as he sank to the floor.

Bjorn could not recall if the man said "Mattick..."

But at this point, Bjorn now wondered if the man who watched him pass out in the hallways of the Convention Center was in fact, Otto Mattick. Did that man take Bjorn's identification, swap it for his own and then run?

Is that why everybody here, in the courtroom of this under-water settlement of Brio, thought Bjorn was Otto Mattick? Bjorn could not be certain and knew he had to quietly do some research to either confirm or disprove his theory.

But how could Bjorn investigate anything tied, as he was, hand and ankles to this defendant's chair?

After a long pause, Zor startled Bjorn when he proclaimed to the court, "I do not think your elaborate story is sufficient for this esteemed court of Brio to believe that you are another person, Mr. Otto Mattick."

Bjorn stared up at the glass dome ceiling of the Brio courtroom, squinting at the sunbeam as his pupils contracted. He kept telling himself he must still be dreaming. In reality, he had already been here much longer than he would have been of his own free will.

Once more, Bjorn took stock of the sights around him: the blank-faced jury with their simple uniforms and dash of gold fabric; the people outside, all wearing the same clothing...

Through the transparent walls of Brio's biosphere, Bjorn observed sea creatures swimming around the enclosed Brio bubble.

Bjorn thought to himself, "I guess I am their pet now." Then he thought, "I will never keep a fish bowl, again." But he said nothing out loud. He merely turned his gaze to Zor.

Fully ensconced in the golden robes

floating around him, Bjorn's flamboyant interrogator Zor glided to Bjorn to lock eyes with him, obviously trying to get a reaction out of the news reporter. Bjorn remained expressionless himself.

Zor swished his full bell sleeves as he pulled the trailing robes behind him with a dramatic swirl. Zor appeared to Bjorn to be a little girl enjoying the feel of the fabric of her mother's gowns when dressing up. Bjorn was curious as to how many robes this Zor owned.

Then, Bjorn wondered how far away he was from Courtly City.

He strained his powerful wrists against the constraints, which were still too tight for his muscular frame. He still could not figure out why he had been made a victim here. Or was Otto Mattick the real victim? Did Bjorn stumble into a scoop of a story, which would make Sammy Scribe, his boss at the Daily Memo, proud?

Bjorn was now beginning to question if it was really so smart to go along with these strange rules. Maybe he could learn something... as long as his life wasn't threatened, that is.

Outside the dome ceiling, fish swam languidly in the azure liquid surrounding the biosphere. Shafts of sunshine reflected off pale blue churning waters, creating a dappled dance of sunspots glinting from the glass walls. But was he really underwater? Or was everything he saw just some technical projection, a deliberate confusion of images designed to keep him off balance?

Bjorn regarded the golden robed man before him and softly said through clenched teeth, "Mattick is not my name. I'm Bjorn Esterday."

Zor leaned very close to Bjorn without touching him.

"You are only to speak when directly addressed by the authorities of Brio, our little underwater village."

Bjorn softly retorted, "And what is your position in the hierarchy of this Brio place?"

Zor replied, "As Zor, I am the rule maker... Prosecutor... Attorney... Mayor... Teacher... Whatever is needed. The authority of Zor supersedes all other powers as is indicated by my robes... save that of Judge Watson," he nervously added as he looked up to the floating balloon head of Judge Watson and bowed deeply to show his subservience as he added with face near the ground, "My Esteemed Bonitor, Judge Watson, sir...".

Bjorn took a deep breath and shook his wrists, still trapped by the restraints on the armrests of the chair, "I have played your trial game. May I please go home, your Zor-ness? You realize if I miss a deadline, my boss at the newspaper will come looking for me... but if you let me go now... I won't say or write a thing. Unless you want me to."

Zor was not amused.

He leaned in closer to Bjorn and whispered so only Bjorn could hear, "Do not insult me with your pitiful negotiations! You agreed to distill your consciousness, Mr. Mattick. I indulged you by letting you spin your wild tale to the jury about pretending to be some reporter in the surface world of Courtly City... Need I remind you that although your transformation was not completed, your condition does not permit you to kill the receptacle of another Brio member. In retribution, we could simply have ejected you into the waters. It is only by Watson's wise determination that you are still alive. But that is merely prolonging the inevitable. Why, you wonder? Obvious!

"For the entertainment of your growing Brio audience. You are lucky we are getting so many viewers."

Zor spun around so fast, his robes swirled upwards to reveal his ankles. In a booming voice he cried out, "Mr. Otto Mattick suffers from the delusion that he is a reporter on the surface. I ask you to consider, Jury of Brio, why is it that when Mr. Mattick was in the transition chamber, next to Mr. Charlie Horse's room, that the next day, Charlie Horse is found dead?"

Bjorn muttered, "I didn't kill some guy I never even met. I've got no motive."

Zor continued, directing his speech to the jury, "As you know, Mr. Horse was having psychological distress issues. He was feeling confined by the clear protective dome of Brio. Mr. Horse was disobeying our rules by reaching out to the former acquaintances of you, the jury. He tried to contact vile polluted surface dwellers, from whom you yourselves sought escape by coming to the sanctuary and solace of Brio in the first place. Is it possible Mr. Otto Mattick wished to stop Charlie Horse from making further contacts on the surface? Or perhaps the defendant was exacting revenge against Charlie for trying to take this woman we keep hearing about away from our defendant?"

The floating head of Watson, the judge, asked Zor, "What was the original plan for dealing with Mr. Charlie Horse's rebellious actions?"

Zor bowed deeply to the balloon and then addressed the Jury. "My solution was to get Charlie Horse to appreciate the vastness of the sea by putting him in an even more confined space. He merely needed something against which to compare our limitless world."

Bjorn glanced up and around thinking to himself that anybody might get claustrophobic being confined in this bubble.

Zor continued, "Charlie Horse was locked in his room each night with a guard posted at the door to ensure his therapy was maintained without interruption. This morning, the guard unlocked the door and found Mr. Horse dead." Zor emphasized his final word with an animated arm gesture, "Stabbed!"

Zor then turned to the balloon face of Judge Watson and asked, "Is this in keeping with Dr. Linden's wishes?"

Bjorn's brow furrowed. Who was Dr. Linden? Why would some Dr. Linden want to influence this trial?

The balloon Judge replied to Zor,

"Never mind Dr. Lou Pole Linden, nor anyone from AromaX. If this defendant, Mr. Otto Mattick follows the rules, keep him alive for the trial. If he steps out of line one centimeter, then eject him into the waters for the sea creatures to feed upon."

Zor spun around to face Bjorn, and spoke with clenched jaw, "Mr. Mattick, during this trial, you will remain silent unless directly questioned."

He took a step closer and leaned down to make eye contact with Bjorn as he continued. "You are forbidden from touching anyone, including the guards. We have eyes everywhere, Mr. Mattick. If you commit even the slightest infraction of our rules, we will have justification to instantly destroy you. Eject you into the waters where all of us can watch your body used as feed for the sea creatures out there... Do you understand these rules? No talking. No touching. Do you understand?"

As if Zor wanted to make his point, he gestured his arm flamboyantly and a guard obeyed his silent command immediately. The guard swooshed to Zor's side, glaring at Bjorn in the same manner.

Bjorn marveled at the sight of this Zor a very small man, fully clad in glittering robes, compared to the much bigger guard, wearing a more austere uniform, but with the same splash of gold incorporated into his garment.

Bjorn wondered if the culture of Brio showed hierarchy by how many sparkles one wore. If that were the measure, Bjorn was clearly at the bottom of this Brio pecking order. He had no golden threads whatsoever.

Bjorn noted that when Zor spied a sunbeam shining down through the dome of underwater Brio, Zor would deliberately step into the light. It was as if he were desperately trying to be the focus, the center of some cheap ostentatious show, delightedly admiring the flamboyance of his own robes, which, to him, glittered like stars in the sky.

"I get your rules," Bjorn said. "Touch a

citizen of Brio and I become fish food. Got it. But, Zor, you in all fairness can agree to let me investigate the accusations made against me so I can fairly present a defense for these allegations of murder, right?"

Zor replied, "I see no need for that, Mr. Mattick."

Bjorn took a deep breath and turned to the jury, "If I am innocent and you condemn me for the murder of Charlie Horse, then you are all trapped in this bubble of trouble with the real murderer roaming around ready to strike down another victim. If I don't succeed in proving my innocence, you can still condemn me." Then Bjorn muttered to himself, "as you obviously already decided to do before this trial even started....so you have nothing to lose...and it could be entertaining..."

The Jury murmured to each other. The balloon head of Watson floated down to confer with Zor.

2 CHAPTER 02: (2030) Cell, Sweet Cell

With a heavy sigh, Zor raised his arm and called, "Seeds!" and then pointed at Bjorn, still restrained in the chair.

The individual named 'Pat Seeds' emerged from the crowd, approached Bjorn, stood next to him, and unlocked Bjorn's wrist restraints by stepping on a foot pedal near the chair. Pat Seeds was careful not to touch Bjorn Esterday. When Bjorn stood up, his legs tingled as feeling was now returning to his limbs. His head pounded and ached, his neck felt stiff.

He stepped away to follow the

shapeless form of Pat Seeds and looked back to where he had been sitting. The other viewers had a definite feminine or masculine form, yet Pat Seeds seemed to be...undecided. Bjorn couldn't tell if this was a male or female.

Zor waved his arms high so the golden fabric of his robes slid down his arms. The jury stood up and vacated their seats in an orderly silent manner and walked out of the room.

"Touching results in immediate execution, Mr. Otto Mattick," Zor tossed over his shoulder as he left the courtroom.

Pat Seeds and Bjorn Esterday stood alone in the courtroom.

Bjorn now became aware of the loud droning hum of the air compressors, which he realized was probably pumping oxygen into this underwater biosphere.

Bjorn's eyes travelled to the larger structure, which had been behind Bjorn's chair, where the balloon head of the judge floated for most of the trial.

Normally, Bjorn would expect a human judge to sit behind a raised bench-like structure such as this. Instead of a chair, Bjorn saw a tiny clear motionless cube positioned on the edge of the bench.

As Bjorn followed Pat Seeds, his new acquaintance, out of the courtroom, Bjorn fixed his gaze on the cube.

He noticed the balloon head of the judge was now deflating as if controlled by the clear glowing cube, which was small enough to fit into his hand. Bjorn wondered if the leader of this underwater village was Watson or if Watson was just a hologram image created by Zor.

It was an odd situation and the only thing Bjorn was sure of was that he was quite awake and this was not a dream.

As Bjorn gazed up at the transparent ceiling he saw sea life swim around the outside of the clear bubble containing this world. His heart felt heavy as he reasoned Sammy Scribe wouldn't start looking for him until after his extended vacation time was up...if at all... He now regretted writing that article about

Watson and hoped printing it would not bring down the wrath of the Administrators. If that article did offend the Courtly City Administrators, would Bjorn lose his job at the Daily Memo? If he lost his job, would Sammy even be allowed to look for his missing reporter?

As Pat Seeds led Bjorn Esterday through transparent hallways, Bjorn wondered who was Dr. Linden? Who was Otto Mattick? Why was Otto being accused of killing a man named Charlie Horse?

Where were these other people? Not in Brio, that was obvious.

Bjorn wondered if those men had been in Brio, would they help

Bjorn? Would they clear up the misunderstanding of mistaken identity? Could they explain that Bjorn was not Otto Mattick and did not kill this Charlie Horse?

Bjorn's heart sank as he realized he could not expect help from anyone down here...wherever 'here' was.

"This way, Mr. Mattick," Pat Seeds said as Bjorn lingered, gazing around the now empty court room. Bjorn nodded and approached Seeds, who immediately stepped back.

Seeds advised, "Careful! Avoid getting too close to me. I am a resident of Brio. Zor has advised you. He is watching I assure you. His orders and consequences have been stated and will remain in effect until the results of this trial are finalized. I am your guardian during your stay. Trial will resume when Zor returns to Brio."

As he followed Pat Seeds, his new keeper, Bjorn thought that now would be the perfect time to make a run for freedom. A brief moment later, however, he realized he had no idea where to go.

Bjorn looked down at the pale blue floors and confirmed ...he was totally alone on this one.

3 CHAPTER 03: (2030) COURTLY CITY: SAMMY'S DAILY MEMO OFFICE: MARIA CARINA –FIND'S BJORN'S REDMAILED WATSON ARTICLE. VIRGINIA HAMM GETS BJORN FIRED

The corporate steel and black floor of Courtly City's last, fact-checked newspaper, the Daily Memo, bustled with its typical, frantic activity.

Reporter Maria Carina burst into Sammy Scribe's office with a panicked look on her face.

Maria Carina's eyes focused on Sammy with a glare as she shouted, "I got the copy from Bjorn's coverage of the Watson motivational speaker at the Courtly City Convention Center. It's been stuck in the RedMail queue for a couple of days."

"Huh," Sammy grunted without looking up from his desk.

"After I read what Bjorn Esterday wrote, I scanned the HIBs which checked into that Watson convention. Do you realize Otto Mattick was there? If you had sent me, I would have interviewed Otto.

Instead, I find out you sent Bjorn? Why, Sammy? Why Bjorn? Why not me?"

"You don't need to interview Otto Mattick on his fall from power. That's old news."

"Why Bjorn?" Maria Carina insisted.

Shrugging his shoulders, Sammy slowly got up from his cluttered desk.

"Bjorn's overworked. I figured a change of pace might help Bjorn's stale writing. Besides, we bowed to a deal. If he could write it up, I'd give him the contact information of a woman he met the day

Jack Courtly died."

Sammy walked to the outer window of his office and gazed down onto the street below before turning back to stand facing Maria Carina.

Maria Carina snapped, "Sammy, you are the Editor- in- Chief of our revered organization. You push back the unreasonable demands of the Top Brass...You know those Administrators are trying to extend their power over the Daily Memo because it is the last reliable communication outlet for the citizens of Courtly. Are you now telling me you're actually running a dating service with your Soldier Police citizen tracking database? Are you?"

Sammy replied, "I keep that SP database a secret... how did you know... never you mind. Look, Bjorn's on vacation right now so..."

Maria shot back, "You know you can only print maybe the first paragraph of what Bjorn wrote. The rest is too opinionated. Did you even read what Bjorn wrote? If you print it, and the

Administrators read it, they could use it as an excuse to over-reach their control of our newspaper and .... Well... they could replace all reporters with some computerized word generator! Sammy, if you print Bjorn's piece on Watson, it could mean layoffs for all of us!

"You can't do it!"

Sammy shook his head, "It's not that bad..."

"Not bad?" Maria Carina stumbled over her words, "Not bad? Let me read what Bjorn wrote: Paragraph 1: One thing became abundantly clear at the Watson-Change-Your-Life convention, held at the Courtly City Convention Center. The people of Courtly City are in pain."

Sammy replied, "See? Just a human interest story."

Maria Carina cleared her throat and continued, "Wait a sec," she smirked, "He goes on to say: They worry. They suffer from stress-induced illnesses. "They feel loss as their efforts to become accepted are often frustrated. They try to cope with loneliness. They try to extinguish their guilt. They are gripped with uncertainty as they recover from the tragic death of Jack Courtly and his immediate family.... I don't think I should read the rest out loud just in case your office is bugged and the Administrators are listening."

At that moment, one of Sammy's worst fears strode confidently into his office with a Soldier Police escort.

He blinked at Virginia Hamm, Administrator, who only made an in person visit if she was about to announce something unpleasant. Maria Carina's eyes grew wide as she tried to hide behind the door the SP had just opened so that Virginia Hamm could enter majestically.

"Administrator Virginia Hamm would like a word with you on the record," the SP escort stated, then stepped aside and closed the door, revealing Maria Carina's hiding place. Maria smiled nervously at the Soldier Police and motioned to Sammy to see if she should stay or leave.

Sammy's expression begged Maria Carina to stay... please don't leave him alone with these people.

Maria Carina reluctantly remained as she noted Sammy Scribe was rendered speechless, frozen.

"Allow me to break the silence, Mr. Scribe..." Administrator Virginia Hamm coolly said with a coy smile. "Did you notice I called you 'Mr.' and not 'Editor' as is your 'Current' title in the Soldier Police Citizen Tracker? Please notice, as well, that 'current' does not mean 'permanent'. "

"Yes, Ma'am," Sammy said, his mouth suddenly dry. His words cracked.

"That is because," Administrator Virginia Hamm continued, "It has come to my attention that one of your reporters has submitted an article for print which casts dispersions..."

"Aspersions," Maria Carina automatically corrected, then clapped her hand to her mouth as Sammy gave her a look of horror.

Administrator Hamm had not heard, and continued, unfazed, "...on one of Courtly City's biggest financial donors to the schools." She ran her finger over Sammy's desk, and impatiently pushed away clutter with a sneer on her face as she added the name, "Watson."

She held out her hand to receive a device proffered by the SP, which would allow Miss Hamm to read aloud, if she wished. It was the intercepted article that Bjorn Esterday had RedMailed days earlier.

Virginia Hamm continued, "Did you know, Mr. Scribe, that with Skipper Courtly replacing Jack Courtly, my jurisdiction has expanded to cover not only all the schools, but communications, as well. That includes this newspaper. Watson grants comfortably large donations to the Administrators, Mr. Scribe. That means if I say we keep Watson happy... I mean it. That is why I no longer will react to printed articles, but will intercept articles submitted via RedMail before they are printed. Did you know one of your reporters... a... Bjorn

Esterday... has written ... uh, wrote... about Watson while Watson's Change-Your-Life convention was in town?"

Sammy squirmed. The soldier police officer took an intimidating step closer toward Sammy.

Virginia Hamm fanned herself as if she were too warm in Sammy's stuffy office, then she said, "The first two sections are fine... But from paragraph three on...Have you read this?" she cleared her throat before she spoke aloud, "Paragraph 3: Watson, a motivational speaker travelling across all the corporate cities, is selling hope and second chances. A new life free from pain, sorrow and tragedy. "

Sammy Scribe interrupted, "You know Bjorn's investigations and reports have really made a positive impact on Courtly City. When the wild horses migrated toward the city looking for food, Bjorn wrote a story on it and that got people interested in supporting the Overflow Barn, which takes in retired horses and resells them."

Virginia Hamm snapped, "I'm not interested in saving animals on some used-horse lot, Mr. Scribe. I'm interested in what you may print, which could make generous donors halt their donations to my projects..."

Maria Carina, unable to hold back, interrupted. Her words tumbled like an avalanche, "But, the wild horses broke the fence and got onto the busy roads. Twenty of them. They almost died from being hit by high velocity wheeled vehicles. Bjorn halted traffic that day to save them. He quickly organized volunteers to round up the wild horses and got an Earth Farmer to train them and made contact with the Overflow Barn to make sure there was a place people could put horses they no longer needed. That gave Sammy the opening to talk with Jack Courtly to get us our own stables. The genius of having each reporter assigned to a horse means we can still cover stories during ACAs. It all started because of Bjorn caring for the plight of the horses and now they have a home... with us."

The SP spoke sharply, "There are no wheeled vehicles permitted on the roads during Anti Corporate Activity. We Soldier Police are the only ones allowed to halt traffic and we only do that when there is a terrorist threat from an ACA."

Maria Carina defended her coworker.

"Bjorn got the OK from one of the Soldier Police. I guess Bjorn knows which SPs are not stuffy ...."

Sammy Scribe cleared his throat firmly to get Maria Carina to stop talking.

Ignoring Sammy, Maria Carina quickly added, "Ok, so how about we don't print Bjorn's story and just cover what is happening in AromaX. We could investigate how the Twins managed to take total control of the Board of Directors in AromaX and take over the city so quickly.... You know, find out what's happened to Otto Mattick and..."

Sammy Scribe shot her a pleading look and Maria Carina bit her lip and looked down.

Virginia Hamm dismissed Maria Carina's suggestion, "The Daily Memo mission should really be to focus on fun stories occurring in Courtly City only. No need to worry about incurring travel expenses to investigate some story in another corporate city."

The SP added, "Whatever agreement Editor Sammy Scribe made with Jack Courtly is voided, now that he has died and his brother, Skipper, has taken over."

Sammy declared, "Voided? The horse stable permits for reporters is voided? Why? If the ACA won't let us use wheeled vehicles, why can't we use four-legged transportation?"

The SP replied, "Skipper Courtly, Jack's older brother, is now in charge of Courtly City. I'm sure you will see a request to reduce overhead...like that caused by caring for horses, such as in spending money for a stable and the supplies and personnel needed to maintain these Daily Memo stables."

Maria Carina blurted out, "Bjorn

Esterday was even going to do a series about adding a horse lane to main roads. It would allow the Earth Farmers a way to travel into the city...it would encourage more people to ride horses. You know, we could even investigate the possibility of collecting the manure to convert into fertilizer or use it as another source of energy to sell to other corporate cities, and..."

Virginia Hamm smiled and without looking at Maria Carina coolly said, "You need to stop talking, now, dear."

Sammy piped up, "My reporter, there, Maria Carina, brings up a good point. Our newspaper is a great way of informing the public and getting them excited about positive change. Very uplifting stuff..."

The SP escort to Virginia Hamm held up his hand. "Administrator Virginia Hamm is speaking. Your job is to listen."

Virginia Hamm smiled at the SP and blew him a kiss.

Virginia Hamm's face then turned stern

as she stepped toward Sammy Scribe.

"I don't care how much your reporter likes furry animals. Here is where the story we intercepted in your RedMail turns sour.

"Paragraph 4: 'Watson's hope does have a price tag.' Sammy defended the quoted text.

"Isn't it the Daily Memo's duty, Miss Hamm...um...Administrator Hamm..., to alert the citizens of Courtly City if they are about to be fleeced? I mean Watson promotes a better future without any details. Our reporters have tracked Watson in different Corporate Cities and one thing is constant. Somebody signs up. They disappear. Their bank accounts are suddenly owned by Watson's organization. We don't know where these people are being kept.

"Family and friends never hear from them again and when pushed, Watson gets them to say they are in such a state of bliss they could never go back to their old life."

Virginia Hamm scoffed, "You, Mr. Scribe, are permitting the Daily Memo to print lies. I myself use Watson's materials and techniques to help with training Courtly's teachers."

Sammy Scribe's face reddened.

"My reporters check their facts before anything goes to print. Miss Hamm, I ask you, do you really want some organization funding your school projects if the way they get that money is by conning naïve citizens out of their hard earned credits? Wouldn't that hurt the students in your schools when their parents suddenly go broke or disappear?"

The SP stepped forward and blocked Sammy Scribe.

Maria Carina quietly opened the door and slipped out of Sammy's messy office.

Maria Carina dashed across to her coworkers to alert them about what was happening. Sammy could see through the window of his office that the outer floor, where the reporters worked, was getting quiet and faces were turning toward him.

Virginia Hamm, slowly stepping toward Sammy, continued, "I want to read all of your precious Bjorn Esterday's story to you so you fully understand what I will have the authority to do next..."

She cleared her throat. The SP firmly walked Sammy Scribe back to his chair and with a heavy gloved hand, pushed Sammy down and twisted the chair to face Virginia Hamm.

Virginia Hamm continued, "Sammy Scribe... Please know that I am a career girl and I simply need to be cognizant to the way of which I look to my superiors."

Sammy wished Maria Carina, standing right outside the door, was still present in the room to offer further corrections to the Administrator's random vocabulary.

Administrator Hamm went on...

"Let me continue with Bjorn's story. Paragraph 5: When you first enter a Watson convention, you will be greeted by smiles."

Sammy interjected, "See? That's a positive thing. We are not offending Watson's brand."

Virginia Hamm read further.

"Once you are screened and hand over your HIB, you will be given a convention identification badge. Next, you will have ample opportunity to purchase a myriad of Watson merchandise items.

"Then, when it is time to listen to this speaker, you will hear easy-to- recall phrases, chanted by the audience. The ones I heard were 'embrace the erase' and 'enhance my chance'....and 'Improve me with my ImpMi'. Any attendee can immediately discern Watson has a penchant for rhyming slogans spoken in enthusiastic undulation. He dispenses tasty morsels of 'dreams-come-true' to ravenous audiences eager to consume. He offers his flock of disciples the chance to experience a panacea, which will obliterate all their past mistakes, giving them an exciting new life they never thought they could have."

Sammy spoke up quickly, "Administrator Hamm, I would argue that what Bjorn wrote there would help Watson get more customers."

Virginia Hamm corrected Sammy.

"They are not customers. They are devoted souls committed to improving themselves with what Watson is teaching them."

Sammy replied, "But if Watson was so interested in coaching them to a better life, why don't we even know what the products are... I don't know what an ImpMi is. Nobody does. But I do know citizens who have purchased the ImpMi seem to never be seen again and then after some investigation we have discovered that their bank accounts are now in Watson's organization's name."

Virginia Hamm froze with a beauty pageant smile and shook her head as if Sammy just didn't get it, as she read, "Here is Bjorn's Paragraph 6: Can we really be so egotistical to think we could control every aspect of our lives? Do we not need to submit to the roles we play

74

in life? To our bosses, our friends and family? Would it not be better for us to learn to discuss our problems, to decry compromises, and then focus on our relationship's good qualities?"

Out on the Reporters' Floor, reporters were clustering around Maria Carina. Workers started to pull things off their desks and print out work they had been correcting. They could see the signs.

Virginia Hamm coolly continued to read aloud.

"Paragraph 7: If you enjoy the prospect of running away from your problems and starting over, then Watson is for you. If you enjoy being in a crowd chanting one permitted opinion, come on over. You will be reminded frequently that there is a cost for this brand of salvation. This convention is brimming with aggressive sales staff trained in the most current marketing techniques." Virginia Hamm paused, "Now, I sense a sarcastic tone in that. Before I continue, perhaps you had better summon your Bjorn Esterday."

Smiling, Sammy said, "I can't. See, he

RedMailed that article and then went on his much deserved holiday. I have no idea where he is."

Virginia Hamm looked at her SP and asked, "Is there any way we can track him?"

The SP tapped some buttons on his uniform and looked at the screen in his visor as he reported, "The Watson team has cleared out of Courtly City. I do see that a Bjorn Esterday tried to buy a ticket at the train station the day the convention ended, but that is where our system stops tracking him."

Virginia Hamm turned back toward Sammy Scribe. "Fine. We'll wait for him to return, then."

Sammy added, "You know," he looked at the SP, "I've interviewed other SPs who have had family disappear into Watson's world and they want to get their loved ones back. I know there are some SPs who would want this published."

Although Sammy could not see inside

the closed visor of the SP, he did see the helmet tilt down as if the man inside the uniform was thinking, considering what Sammy had just said. The SP sighed heavily. Sammy understood. This man in uniform was totally owned by the management level above him and no matter what he believed, he had to follow orders...and in this case, the orders of Miss Virginia Hamm, Administrator...the Top Brass.

Virginia Hamm continued to lecture Sammy.

"Mr. Scribe, listen here to your Bjorn Esterday's conclusion: 'Simply accept the fact that you will be seen as a source of profit by this prophet 'Watson'. You will pay to hear that every one of your problems will be remedied if you simply lose weight, take more control over your life, get rich, and find love...all for an easy-to-follow payment plan, which will attach directly to your credits. According to my calculations, such donations will contribute millions to Watson's personal wealth allotment. Remember that all Watson donations are a perfectly legal way for Mr. Watson himself to fleece his flock.' "

Sammy replied, "Oh, you're concerned about the word 'fleecing' ... well... we could come up with another way to convey that Watson is taking advantage of innocent people, and if the SPs can't stop it then our reporters have to alert the people so they can protect themselves."

Virginia Hamm asked, "Is that your opinion, Mr. Scribe, or your reporter's opinion?"

"I think," Sammy said gruffly, "that you are respecting money without thought as to how Watson amasses that money."

Virginia Hamm replied in treacly sweet tones, "I'll ignore that insubordinate comment, Mr. Scribe."

Sammy shot back, "It is only insubordinate if I worked for you. I don't. This paper is kept alive because Skipper Courtly's son, Pip, loves it. As it is. Printed on paper. I work for him."

Realizing Sammy was telling the truth, Virginia Hamm's face became an angry red hue as she spat out the remainder of Bjorn's article for Sammy to hear.

"In this reporter's opinion," Virginia Hamm sarcastically read aloud, "should you wish to partake in a less expensive form of entertainment, consider a trip to our Courtly City library."

Virginia rolled her eyes as she tried to imitated Bjorn Esterday's voice. She cleared her throat and continued, "Mrs. Libris can direct you to any subject which might interest you. Should you wish to calm your aching heart and erase the mistakes of your past, try approaching the person you offended and make sincere restitution."

Virginia paused and muttered that she was always the victim and was justified in placing blame on others. Then she resumed her mocking tone as she read.

"Should you wish to locate a Supreme Being to worship, visit the church in your local community of Earth Farmers. Any one of the Earth Farmers would be happy to set aside harvesting our organic crops, which make the Courtly area famous among all the corporate cities, and pray with you to the God they worship."

Virgina Hamm scoffed at the notion yet persisted in her derisive tone, "The last option is not only cost effective, but it would honor the memory of our leader who worked so hard to establish relations between the citizens of Courtly Corp and the Earth Farmers to profitably export fresh nutritious chemical-free food to other cities.."

Virginia spat that any reference to Jack Courtly, the deceased leader is disrespectful to the current glorious leader, Skipper Courtly. She sneered as she read the rest of the article, "Any one of these options is cheaper and more effective than attending the sinking ship known as the Watson Change Your Life Conference. Anyway we both know this fad will probably end when Watson leaves Courtly City."

With arched eyebrow, Virginia's laser

focus fixated on Sammy Scribe with a final comment, "Watson donates generously. This article smeared his name and cut into possible profits which could have been directed toward my causes."

Sammy noticed that the SP had released his grip on Sammy's shoulder and was moving away toward the door. Sammy stood and said, "So what happens if I print that?"

Virginia Hamm walked toward the door as the SP opened it for her. She then pivoted toward Sammy Scribe and spoke in a loud voice so all the reporters on the floor could hear.

She said, "Right now, Mr. Scribe... if you still want to be known as 'Editor Scribe' in the SP citizen tracker database, you are to un-employ Bjorn Esterday."

Sammy exclaimed, "You want me to just tell him he's fired for no reason?"

Virginia narrowed her gaze, "No!" she breathed with forced control to harness her volcanic anger, "No more communication with Bjorn Esterday! You may not assist him in getting a new job. You are not to notify him of his new unemployed status. He will find out when he returns." She smiled as she continued with her spur of the moment inspiration. "Oh, and your lady reporter who was just in here should leave all AromaX matters alone. The Twins have their hands full with reorganizing that city. It is none of our concern!"

Maria Carina, mouth open, just stared at Virginia Hamm from across the hall.

Virginia Hamm sniffed and added, "I don't want to catch anybody trying to contact any of the Matticks, nor to annoy the Twins of AromaX. In fact, none of your reporters, Mr. Scribe, should interview Otto Mattick or any of the Mattick family. That goes for here in Courtly City, or their home city of AromaX , or any other corporate city. Just stay far away."

The SP whispered something into the ear of Administrator Virginia Hamm.

Inhaling sharply, as if she had almost

forgotten, Virginia Hamm turned toward Sammy Scribe and added loudly, "All Daily Memo horses must go to the Overflow Barn."

Sammy protested, "How are the reporters supposed to get to a story location during an ACA if we lock up the horses?"

Virginia reminded him "Your reporters can walk. Two-legged transportation works just as well as four-legged transportation during the next ACA. Need I remind you that no wheeled vehicles are allowed during ACAs. "

With sudden inspiration, Virginia Hamm added, "Oh, I also expect you to reduce staff overhead by ...shall we start with 20% reduction? Let's see how that goes... Oh, and that is only if you do NOT print this story. I expect your reporter staff to avoid creating similar stories in future. If you did decide to print Bjorn Esterday's story, you can expect the Daily Memo to be fully shut down. I'll convince Skipper and Pip Courtly myself...in my own way... The choice is...of course, yours to make. This is a free city, after all.

"You have until morning to decide."

Virginia Hamm smugly sashayed out with her SP escort. The entire reporting staff silently watched her leave the building before they burst into a cacophony of bustling discussion about what had just transpired.

Sammy sighed as he realized Bjorn was on vacation and Sammy had no way to notify Bjorn to let him know Bjorn had no job to come home to.

Sammy Scribe felt a headache coming on, "This is going to be more difficult than a war, pandemic, economic depression"

Virginia Hamm suddenly called him on his comm. He answered and saw her looking right at him on the screen. "Need I remind you, that your paper is only in business because you print only happy stories."

Sammy's mouth went dry as he replied

to Virginia Hamm's digital image, "I understand, Ma'am. I assure you I have not allowed any or my reporters to print stories on a city going bankrupt and getting sold to a corporation..."

The transmission blinked, as Virginia Hamm reminded Sammy, "Courtly City remains in power because we got rid of gasoline and oil for energy. Those old fuels are not the only thing the AnCors can scrape together to power those old smelly vehicles."

Sammy nodded obediently, "I understand, Miss Hamm. It is an honor to be a citizen of Courtly City which provides the citizens with the best strongest Soldier Police force, which monitor every citizen to ensure compliance and give us the security that you can hear all our thoughts no matter where you are. That is why you called me, I assume."

"So, reminded us both of your duty, Editor Scribe."

Sammy's mouth went dry, "This is why it is my duty to never print about a public figure stealing from the funds set aside for public use... Why there is no inflation. Ever. When prices go up, it just is an opportunity for the people to be more disciplined in spending." He blinked quickly as she gazed at him in slience, expecting more.

Sammy continued, "because celebrities such as yourself, only act on behalf of the people and respect our privacy. You would never take funds for your own personal use. I am honored to have somebody like you in charge, Miss Hamm..."

She smiled, satisfied and ended transmission.

Sammy sighed, relieved and slumped into a nearby chair to recover.

4 What Just Happened?

Bjorn Esterday, reporter for the Daily Memo newspaper of Courtly City, took an assignment from his boss, Sammy Scribe, Editor, to cover a motivational speaker at the Courtly City Convention Center. His plans were to look up the alluring Sarah Paradise, School Teacher, and then head out for a well-deserved holiday.

Bjorn's easy assignment took an unexpected turn and Bjorn found himself on trial in an underwater courtroom, accused of assuming an identity of which Bjorn knew nothing about.

During Bjorn's absence and unbeknownst to Bjorn, he was fired by the School Administrator, Virginia Hamm, for writing an unflattering piece about her department.

Bjorn's instinct to dig deeper until he got the full story was weakened. Bjorn's boss, Sammy Scribe, wanted to keep the newspaper alive. To do this Sammy Scribe put investigative reporter Bjorn on some easy assignments. Neither Sammy nor Bjorn knew that Bjorn's sharp investigative journalistic instincts would both irritate the powerful, and keep Bjorn alive...surviving...or would it?

He knew the Twins gained influence by negative propoganda regarding the leadership in power. He knew they pounded on the lies until the people couldn't discern truth from fiction. But he knew he could never say anything because the Twins still had power.

Which is more deadly? The truth or the powerful who want to conceal the truth?

5 Did You Know...

To test how a small community of people would survive socially in space, some organizations have built 'biosphere domes' to replicate Space Exploration Simulation. Organizations engaged in research regarding 'outer space' have funded on-land domes as valuable training opportunities for future astronauts.

Although there are other "Mars simulation" projects all over the globe, it is thought that volcanic terrains provide rugged landscapes similar to that of Mars.

One example was a dome like structure of about 1,200 square feet.   The occupants were to have no contact with outside people in order to simulate living on Mars. This is to support the directive to put humans on an asteroid in the 2020's and to put humans on Mars in the 2030's.

In the 1990's, another Biosphere was created to mimic a greenhouse. It was built in Arizona.   The goal for the occupants was to grow their own food and recycle the air inside the sealed transparent enclosure.

The 1990's experiment did not succeed as the levels of Carbon Dioxide rose too high to sustain plants and animals. Internal strife amongst the crew resulted in petty squabbles.   After two years, bonding amongst the crew did not occur.

6 Vocabulary

This fictional series introduces some words unique to this world. Also used are standard terms which we encourage you to investigate in a dictionary for your own edification. A consolidated full list of vocabulary for all GONE books is located in the Conversation Station supplemental book.

Bonitor This is the monitor where Zor's boss, Watson's face, is projected on the surface of the balloon as it floats around. The balloon has a camera device where Watson can see what the balloon sees.

Overflow Barn Groomsman The Groomsman is the person to takes care of the horses. The overflow barn is the place in Courtly City where wild or abandoned horses are rounded up and then later sold to buyers who will own the horses and care for them in their own stables. Since the ACA, or the Anti Corporate Activity alert which informs the citizens of Courtly City that AnCor threat is nearby, bans all wheeled vehicles, using a horse for transportation is the only legal mode of moving around Courtly City during an ACA, which has lately become more frequent.

Mayfounder Foundation This is a favorite company of Skipper Courtly, the current ruler of Courtly City and the brother of Jack Courtly. It is unclear what it does but Skipper supports "research" with dedication. Jack does not like the company. It is explained in the book series EDGES.

Skipper Courtly is the current ruler of Courtly City. His formal title is Director of the Courtly City Corporation. His younger brother, Jack Courtly, was ruler before Jack and his family had a terrible train accident (described in EDGES). After the accident, Skipper became ruler of Courtly City.

wrangler a profession which collects horses from the wild and brings them to the barn to be domesticated or trained so they can be sold.

HIB Holographic Image Badge.

ACA Anti-Corporate Activity. The ACA is sounded publicly by the SPs when their sensors pick up the presence of the AnCors. When an ACA alert is in progress, no wheeled vehicles are permitted on the pathways. This is to allow the SPs on horseback to chase the offender. For the citizens, the only mode of transportation available to them during an ACA is anything without a wheel-on-the-streets. The permitted vehicles include trains, horses, or any other mode of transportation not normally used on the street. Since the AnCors use older gasoline-powered cars and trucks, the SPs know that if those are on the road, then there are probably AnCors operating those vehicles. They become an easy target for the SPs.

AnCor Anti-Corporatists. This group has many chapters, but the one located in Courtly City at the time of this writing is led by Percy Snatcher, who relies on his subordinate, Slash, to carry out his orders. This group started as a protest against the increasing power of corporations, but bit by bit, the members were cut off from societal resources by the very corporations they tried to fight. As a result, those who are members of the AnCors, at the time of this writing, live "off the grid" of the corporate kingdom. They use older technologies of the past, now abandoned by the citizens of the corporate city. They also have learned to survive by selling their mercenary talents to the highest bidder, which, hypocritically, embodies the very spirit of "anything for a profit" which they claim they are trying to combat in formal corporations.

Earthie This is a derogatory term used to refer to a member of the Earth Farmer Community. The Earth Farmers are a group of people who eschew the technology of the modern world in Courtly City and instead quietly and peacefully live and hone their farming and other hand-craft skills, including but not limited to quilting.

Earthshake An archaic translation would be earthquake. This is a term referring to the shaking of the ground which, at times, fractures the ground to the point of opening fissures.

Redmail (Deadmail) This is a term for redacted mail received electronically. RED = Redacted Electronic Document. Deadmail is a nickname given by those in Courtly City because at times the document is so redacted that there is no readable meaningful content.

ipsa scientia *potestas* est   This is a Latin term used by Mrs. Libris, the Librarian. The phrase was penned by Francis Bacon in 1597. Some translate it to mean "Knowledge itself is power" which Mrs. Libris applies by encouraging the children from Miss Paradise's class to become powerful, honest, honorable citizens armed with factual truth.

SP   Soldier Police which are the armed enforcement body assigned to each corporate kingdom, such as Courtly.

Twins   This is a term referencing a faceless power figure who replicated lies until lesser power figures copied that leader's brand or habits for the sole purpose of gaining power. Followers sacrificed their reputation, integrity, and boldly lied. The Twins encourage in-fighting for the leader's favor, back-stabbing, gas-lighting, and other destructive behaviors to obtain wealth and power at any cost.

ABOUT Wynter Sommers

Wynter Sommers is the pseudonym for an American writing team, which harnesses multiple skills in technology, research, history and education. Formally trained with a PhD in Education, Wynter Sommers blends academic classroom experience, with corporate sophistication, and a passion for developing more effective student insights through engaging storytelling.

Wynter Sommers has a heart to inspire creativity and develop critical thinking skills, all to encourage readers to make wise choices in life.

Wynter Sommers takes each story and weaves the plot with classic gripping elements, which endure throughout repeated readings, revealing new meanings each time the story is explored. The small choices a reader makes in real life could have a lasting effect in future generations. This set of stories shows the origin of not just Bjorn Esterday and Sarah Paradise, but of their ancestors and the sort of world which was established, which unfolded in each generation until Bjorn and Sarah met.

It is rewarding to learn of heartfelt, thought provoking conversations taking place globally about the characters of these books. Should the reader be presented with extraordinary circumstances, it is the sincerest wish that they act with honor, truth and integrity to overcome obstacles in real life whilst the reader hones skills of self-reliance and collaborative teamwork despite barriers outside of the reader's control. Wynter Sommers hopes you enjoy the other ***Bjorn Esterday Was not Born Yesterday*** stories in this series.

www.ingramcontent.com/pod-product-compliance
Lightning Source LLC
Chambersburg PA
CBHW051841020726
47502CB00005B/1895